To Betsy's kids
I hope you like
my book.

Love, Ann McGovern
October 16, 1997

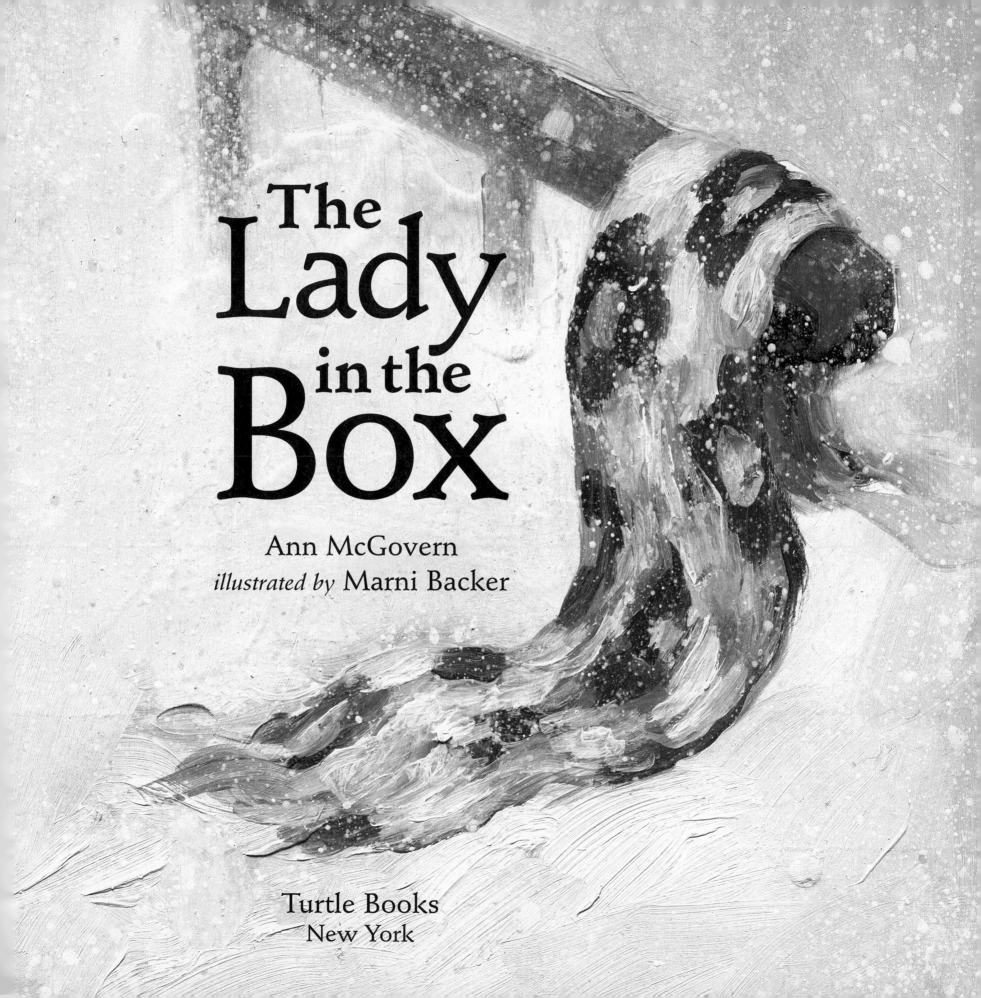

The Lady in the Box

Ann McGovern

illustrated by Marni Backer

Turtle Books
New York

For my friends at Goddard-Riverside Community Center,
especially Bernie Wohl —and—
For my friends at Sponsors for Educational Opportunity,
especially Michael Osheowitz — AM

For Kelly — MB

Turtle
B O O K S

The Lady in the Box
Text copyright © 1997 by Ann McGovern
Illustrations copyright © 1997 by Marni Backer

First Published in 1997 by Turtle Books

Turtle Books, 866 United Nations Plaza, Suite 525
New York, New York 10017

Cover and book design by Jessica Kirchoff Bowlby
Text of this book is set in Stempel Schneidler medium
Illustrations are rendered in oil

First Edition
Printed on 80# Evergreen matte natural, acid-free paper
Smyth sewn, cambric reinforced binding
Printed and bound in the United States of America

10 9 8 7 6 5 4 3 2 1

Library of Congress Cataloging-in-Publication Data
McGovern, Ann.
The lady in the box / Ann McGovern ; illustrated by Marni Backer.   p.   cm.
Summary: When Lizzie and Ben discover a homeless lady living in their neighborhood, they must
reconcile their desire to help her with their mother's admonition not to talk to strangers.
ISBN 1-890515-01-9 (hardcover : alk. paper)
[1. Homeless persons—fiction. 2. Helpfulness—Fiction. 3. Neighborhood—Fiction.]
I. Backer, Marni, ill. II. Title. PZ7.M478485Lad 1997 [E]—dc21 97-13633 CIP AC

Distributed by Publishers Group West

ISBN 1-890515-01-9

There was a lady who slept in a box down our street.

Before dark, she sat in her box in front of the Circle Deli.

She just sat and stared.

When the sky got black, she curled up in her box. I think she slept in the box all night.

She must have liked the Circle Deli because of the warm air from the basement that came through the grate. The warm air kept her from freezing.

I never saw her in the morning. My sister Lizzie didn't either. She probably folded up her box and put it some-where safe till nighttime.

We could have kept it for her in our house. But Lizzie and I aren't supposed to talk to strangers. So we didn't offer.

She looked like a kind, nice lady. I smiled at her. Just yesterday, I thought she smiled back. Maybe she didn't. Maybe I just wished she had.

The lady in the box looked hungry.

It was Lizzie's idea to bring her food. I reminded Lizzie that we can't talk to strangers. Lizzie said we wouldn't talk to her. We'd just put some crackers and peanut butter next to her box.

The first time, we forgot the knife for putting peanut butter on the crackers. But she managed somehow. The next day the peanut butter jar was empty.

I thought she should eat food that was good for her. So I brought her two raw carrots, a bunch of celery, and an apple.

Lizzie said the lady in the box didn't have many teeth, not enough for chewing hard food. There were a couple of cans of soup in our kitchen cabinet. Cream of celery and vegetable noodle. Soft and mushy soups. Just right for someone without teeth.

Lizzie thought vegetable noodle was better. I thought celery. We had a fight about it. Lizzie won.

We heated up the vegetable noodle soup and ran down the stairs fast to get it to her before the soup got cold. Then we ran home before Mama could tell we were up to something again. Mama says we are always up to something.

The store windows were all Christmasy. It got dark early and the nights were very cold.

The lady in the box didn't have warm-enough clothes.

We looked in our closets.

On Lizzie's shelf was a big warm scarf with bright red flowers.

Lizzie said she didn't like the scarf because it was so itchy.

I wasn't so sure the lady in the box would like it either. But it was better than the cold wind blowing on her neck.

We left it outside her box.

Later we saw the scarf wrapped around her neck.

Maybe she likes red flowers.

She called after us, "My name is Dorrie. Thanks."

"My name is Lizzie," Lizzie said. "My brother is Ben. And you're welcome."

I was worrying about Mama's rule about speaking to strangers.

"Now that we know her name, she's not exactly a stranger," I said to Lizzie. She nodded.

The next day it was freezing cold.

The owner of the Circle Deli came out of his store.

"Get away from here," he shouted at Dorrie. "I don't want you sitting in front of my store anymore. People are complaining."

Dorrie had to move. She set up her box in front of an empty store down the street. But no warm air came up from the basement there. She began to shiver. Her lips looked sort of blue.

Lizzie said it was about ten degrees above zero.

"We have to do something," Lizzie said, "or she'll freeze to death."

"We could bring her some of our blankets," I said.

"That's dumb," Lizzie said. "Mama would find out for sure."

We were quiet as we climbed the two flights
of stairs to our apartment.

I figured Lizzie was thinking about the same
thing I was thinking about.

Telling Mama or not telling Mama.

But when we got home, it was Mama who told us a thing or two.

It's not easy to fool Mama.

Why were the cans of soup missing, she wanted to know. Why was the flowered scarf gone?

She asked us what we were up to.

We decided to tell her. Maybe if she met the lady in the box, she would know how to help her better.

So we told Mama about her and how we gave her the food, starting with the peanut butter and crackers. And how she had to move her box away from the Circle Deli. And that her name was Dorrie and she was freezing cold.

Mama didn't get mad and yell at us. Instead, she sighed and said, "Okay, let's see your lady in the box."

The three of us went downstairs and around the corner.

Mama knocked on the box.

"Come on out," she said in her no-nonsense tone of voice. "I want to meet you."

Dorrie opened the top flap of the box and sat up. Mama has this amazing way of making people talk to her.

Dorrie started to talk to us. She told us about losing her job and not being able to pay her rent so she had to leave her apartment. She said she tried to stay in a shelter for homeless women but someone there stole her bag of clothes while she was sleeping. After that, she slept in a box on the street.

Mama got that look on her face. It was her I'm-going-to-do-something-about-it look.

Mama marched to the Circle Deli. We had to run to catch up.

When she saw the owner, Mama began to give it to him. She said that Christmas was coming soon and that it was freezing cold outside and she used words like human kindness and simple charity until he said, "Okay, okay, she can stay."

We told Dorrie she could move her box back to
the Circle Deli where it was warm.
She smiled a big smile!

We climbed up to our apartment but all I could think about was helping Dorrie. But how?

When Mama came in to kiss me goodnight, I told her I wanted to help Dorrie more but I didn't know how to do it.

Mama said she'd think of something and go to sleep now, honey.

When Saturday came, Mama asked us if we
wanted to help in the neighborhood soup kitchen.
"Homeless people get free lunches there," she said.

The soup kitchen was in a church basement.
The line to get in was long. I felt sad that there
were so many people needing free soup.

My job was to put a piece of bread and a pat of butter on a paper plate. Lizzie's job was to hand the plate to the people in line. Mama's job was dishing out cup after cup of soup.

I was so busy doing my job that I almost didn't hear my name being called.

I looked up to see Dorrie in line. She smiled at me.

"Hello, Ben," she said quietly.

"Hi, Dorrie," I said, smiling back.

"Who's your friend?" the helper next to me asked.

Friend! Nobody ever called Dorrie my friend before. It sounded nice.

Maybe someday, I thought, Dorrie wouldn't have to live in her box. Maybe she could get a job and a place of her own. She'd have a key just like I have a key to our apartment.

I reached into my pocket and took out my lucky key ring. It has a plastic four-leaf clover on it.

I took off my key and I gave my new friend Dorrie the key ring with the four-leaf clover.

Maybe it would bring her luck.

Maybe someday she could use it for her very own key.

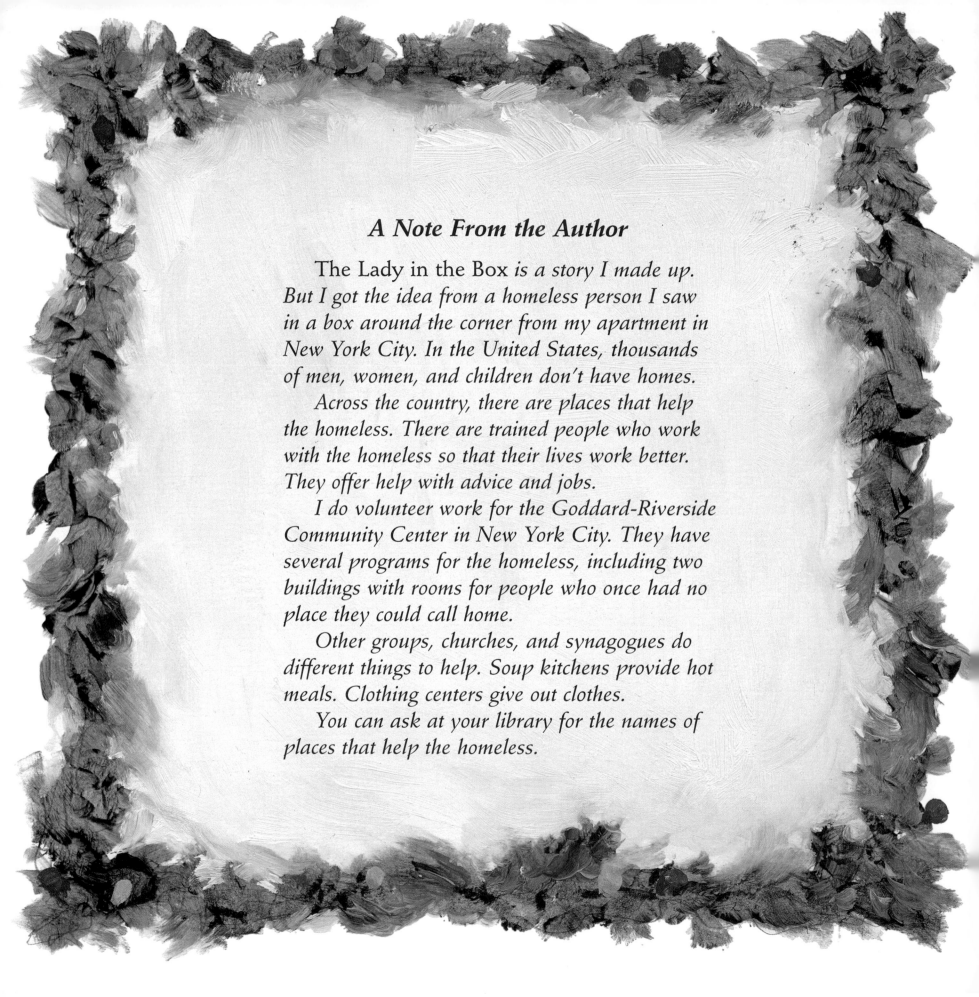

A Note From the Author

The Lady in the Box *is a story I made up. But I got the idea from a homeless person I saw in a box around the corner from my apartment in New York City. In the United States, thousands of men, women, and children don't have homes.*

Across the country, there are places that help the homeless. There are trained people who work with the homeless so that their lives work better. They offer help with advice and jobs.

I do volunteer work for the Goddard-Riverside Community Center in New York City. They have several programs for the homeless, including two buildings with rooms for people who once had no place they could call home.

Other groups, churches, and synagogues do different things to help. Soup kitchens provide hot meals. Clothing centers give out clothes.

You can ask at your library for the names of places that help the homeless.